A TIME to Go In

Iexsheev Giovanni Hickman

Published by
G Creative Works
Memphis, Tennessee
Linktr.ee/gcreativeworks

ISBN   978-1-716-52227-7 (e-book)
ISBN   978-0-578-87517-0 (paperback)
Library of Congress Control Number: 2021904982

Cover Designer: fiverr.com/rose_miller
Interior Desiger: NuancePublishing.com
Technical Editors: G Creative Works, fiverr.com/kimberlyrose90

General – Historical Fiction

Printed in the United States of America

Contents

This book is dedicated to my children, the building of a renewed legacy for my future generations, my mom and dad, Deloris and Clifford Sr. Peterson, and to all my sisters and brothers with much love.

Acknowledgements

I give special honor to the Creator and the Ancestors for bestowing such gifts on me to come forward and share my uniqueness with the world.

About the Author

I simply live and in-joy the simple things in life, such as nature walks, books, international arts, music & dances. I also in-joy writing, learning, and being in the company of my loved ones and genuine people, supporting local businesses and a variety of culture and community events. I love traveling, especially road trips and trying different international food dishes. I honor this privilege of motherhood journey with two beautiful children and we love cooking mostly, tasty healthy vegan, and vegetarian food dishes. My blog is Minding Wealth at **minditdotblog.wordpress.com. The motto is: "The mind is a natural resource, so mind well."** I've earned an A.S. in Business Administration at Southwest Tennessee Community College;

B.B.A. in Management Information Systems at The University of Memphis; and a Master of Accountancy at Belmont University; and licensed as a tax practitioner.

Well-being affiliated items are available for purchase at **linktr.ee/gcreativeworks.**

Contact Information
Linktr.ee/gcreativeworks
gwrites4@protonmail.com
Instagram @gwrites4

Other Books by the Author
A non-fiction publication to be released in 2022

Introduction

In the early spring of 2020, the day of the earth stood still, but I continued with my daily routine despite the chaos and confusion of this very thing that was spreading globally and affecting the health, minds, and finances of the populations at large. This unpredictable health crisis has brought the movement of global activities, both personal and businesses, to a moment of silence, slowing down the transference of energy among people, places, things, and ideas. When I arrived home at eight o'clock in the night, I sat motionless in my vehicle, smothered by the quietness that surrounded me; yet, I also was beginning to feel a sense of relief. No trains were running on the tracks holding up traffic for a mile long and no high traffic volume noises of trucks, motorcycles, and other transportation modes were flowing from the nearby interstate. In the apartment complex where I live, the parking spaces were at a maximum capacity – everyone was at home. I then stood outside my vehicle to observe the night sky, it was so clear and I began to notice more stars than usual because the aircraft controllers never received any more permissions to leave the grounds. Suddenly, I had an eerie feeling that overwhelmed my body and my mind began conjuring up many negative thoughts about what the potential outcome might be from all the events and reactions to this thing spreading all around the world. I reminded myself that this is not the time to panic, but to seek out more information and learn of the safety measures to implement to protect me and my family. Furthermore, it will be beneficial for the populace to take "a time out" and go into their home spaces and destress from their routine on steroids! After all, I believe that I battle with an addiction to these life imbalances and it is unfortunate that I have imposed these stressful conditions upon my avatar, forcing it to adapt. Pausing in that moment of stillness to focus on my breathing, I then heard the voice within me saying, *"Time with thy self is what I need from you so take what is happening, despite the unknowns and accept this as your gift of time – the year 2020 is a time to go in – to thy self."* The night creatures began singing so loudly that they interrupted the meditation. So then, the stars became seemingly shining brighter than ever and the air started to feel crisp and fresh. Finally, I settled into a feeling of overwhelming joy, concurred with the voice inside, and it then continued in the wisdom it was sharing:

Though the earth seem to be still, nature now will thrive evermore! Just as the children are crying for their parents to be with them at home, parents are also worrying and weeping because the strength to go on cannot be gained from consistently putting out energy that is draining their spirits, in order to provide and make ends meet for their families. Also, the elders are sitting in spaces that hold deep memories of long ago and the effects of loneliness are becoming too much to bear and some are deciding to live on in the afterlife. Everyone is too busy managing their perpetual hamster wheel-like lifestyle. Know that everything that's taking place is not what it might seem. What you might perceive as death is another beginning of a renewed life. As truth history has revealed itself, it was **life** *that our ancestors were obsessed with; they were not obsessed with death.*

Like its creations, the Creator also has personality and the process of creation cannot be respectfully observed nor can knowledge be ascertained when you are heavily immersed in overstimulating activities on a continuous basis. The creatures of the underworld will multiply greater in one day than they had birthed in one week because the waterways are open and free and are not choked up from the pollution emitted by human activities. You see, we are all co-creators dwelling on Mother's Earth property, and in her endless abundance, she hears, sees, and knows all things. Now, it is time for the return of families to be united and sit at the dinner table and have the mental patience to have a real talk with their loved ones. Notwithstanding the fact that everyone needs their own individual space and time to get to know thy self, thy power, and thy uniqueness.

Tears of joy overflowed in that moment of truth being revealed to me while the voice within ceased. Then, I looked to the heavens and motioned a good night gesture of gratitude. We were all inside now, the pantry was stocked, and the residential energy was burning twice as much power, but everyone's countenance showed a sigh of relief from the hustle and bustle of our daily mode of operating. Thereafter, my family and I indulged in a bowl of ramen noodles in a vegan stock mineralized with the Kombu sea vegetable and topped with sautéed mushrooms, red onions, and spinach. Then we were off to the dream spaces, allowing our avatars to rest in the night as the healthy lite meal we ate ensured that we have sweet dreams. I, on the other hand, was not ready to enter into other worlds unknown. I had other ideas that were forthcoming and those thoughts needed to be examined. Otherwise, I would have been preparing the items we needed to utilize for the next day and packed lunches. I have been enjoying the job role's assignments; however, the work just fascinated me whenever I sat quietly in the office and just looked at it for hours. Even though I laughed at the thought of this, I must confess that it is a true story, and I remembered the playwright who said, "Any idiot can get through a crisis. It is this day to day living that wears you out," and my night was onto a smooth start. Seriously, even though I now have these moments to mediate on my circumstances that I have not been happy with and the goals that I have been wanting to achieve, I opened my journal to write those thoughts coming in. These thoughts flooded many pages as if I had intentionally set down to author a book. How I got here was the reoccurring theme I was expressing; a single-parent household, academic degrees and certifications without the equivalent compensation and higher up promotions, another consistently inconsistent partnership, and possessing the knowledge of how to generate riches, but struggling with increasing my financial wealth. Then, I felt this intense energy in the center of my body, from my throat down to my naval, as though my body was tearing and choking up on these truths I have come to know. In truth, the pains and hurts I felt were unbearable. I laid down on the floor stirring up at the ceiling in the overwhelming space and silence until I was blinded with tears.

The next day, I woke up to back pains without a clue as to how long I had been laying there. I did not feel anything as I opened my eyes and had no idea what dreams occupied my mental real estate when I dozed off. Nonetheless, I had awakened at 5:44 a.m. with a blissful feeling and realizing that the opportunity was presented for me to clear my home space and use this gift of time to reflect deeper into my past experiences, and the lessons those experiences came packaged with. Most importantly, I needed to self-correct some things that would then greatly serve me and my family moving forward, especially in the changing of times in this day and age. Altogether, this is the end of something to begin again. However, it is the beginning with a renewed paradigm aligned with intentional actions liking to that of a seed being nourished and attended to properly with love and care, which results in a fruitful supply in its time. So how shall one begin to examine oneself? I haven't really had that conversation with mother about my first early days on this plane of existence, and I am emotionally and mentally available to receive and inquire intelligently because I have come to know that **it is not the number of books that I have read, but the depth of the questions I would ask.** Having said that, I shall mentally prepare to have that conversation because I do not recall having lived many early glory days. So, first, I'll visit the river park and mediate silently by the waters, which helps me with grounding and balancing out the emotions that I'll once again revisit.

Chapter 1

UNLIMITED BEING

After the mediation at the river park, I drove to a trade and used bookstore to browse the new collections which I have always found some pretty interesting books. I have invested enough money at this bookstore to have at least a 10% ownership interest if I could based it on my past purchases. Adjacent to the main entrance are the rare books and I saw a book titled, *"What Mama Couldn't Tell Us About Love."* I assumed someone had the idea to purchase this book and misplaced it, but was it really out of place? I then clasped my hands together giving thanks to the Creator of the Universe for this timely alignment! As I was flipping through the pages, I started having thoughts about the conversation I will have with my mother. I began pondering if initiating this talk would reactivate some emotions better left dormant. I had not been aware if she has ever taken any measures to recover and heal from past wounds. Furthermore, I believe what the author wrote about had spoken to each of our past circumstances, although we experienced different scenarios. So, individually, we should come forward into a form of healing holistically to prepare us to be readily open to receive the abundance that has been piling up. Nevertheless, the author's bolded statement spoke volumes to me that **_learning to love myself has been like trying to draw water from a dry well. My parents didn't love themselves either. My lack of self-love has definitely kept me from forming a healthy relationship. I just wish I had known more about myself and my history before I even looked at a man,_** and I concurred. Personally, I think that there are no coincidences because this book laid in plain sight just for me!

Later that evening, I contemplated on the message I received from the book and decided not to dive deeper into the events that transpired in my first early years. However, my objective was to get an innerstanding of the child I was. Needless to say, that I had been apparently disconnected from the spirit in the child I was, the child I never knew, but I wished I had known her. I can only imagine that she was a curious and happy child and not a melancholy child, always seeking, asking questions, trying to make sense of whatever that she was discovering, exploring, and pondering. What if she was able to experience a balanced childhood? I just wondered how she would be living today, what her level of discernment would have been in choosing her partner and career path? Contrary to that idea, she learned the behaviors of acting in fear and experienced much confusion and chaos, thus, attracting more of the same unwanted behaviors and feelings over her developing years, in which she eventually succumbed to emptiness and loneliness within. Wherever this child may be, she's all grown-up now, and I just wondered if she ever self-recovered and resurrected to the unlimited being of her truth. Once again, these heavy thoughts were weighing on my consciousness and I took a moment to look into the mirror at the reflection of myself. Realizing the truth buried inside can reveal its wisdom when you are ready to become the student, and consequently, I found that the master has always been present to teach. Henceforth, I've recognized that no one is coming to save me, and the freedom, harmony and balance that I desire in my life are all that I must give unto myself! Meanwhile, the night was growing, and I knew that contacting my mother to discuss some things would ease my troubled mind.

Mom always greeted me with "Hello Dear, how are you and the children doing?" and of course, I would express that all was excellent in my world with a vibrant and jovial tone, hiding any sensitivity that I had been feeling before I called. "What's on your mind, Dear," she would say. Then, I said, "Since the outbreak of this thing has granted us all some time to go in, I have been accompanied by my thoughts to revisit my first early years. I have not reached a level of fulfillment in my life, yet, I am grateful for the life of my girls. But there's something I cannot explain that I am seeking. I have meditated on where I am currently in my life progressions, so I believe it would serve me well to also revisit those first early years." She replied, "I can definitely understand that, my Dear. I do know what you mean by all you have said. So what do you want to know?" In a nutshell, I shared with my mother that all I wanted to know was how I behaved as a child, what my interests were, and if there were anything I did consistently or unexpectedly that she formed in her opinion about my natural talents. I wasn't sure how my mother would respond, after all, it was a loaded question, but it was also straightforward without reviving any other events that had occurred that I would rather not discuss. The toxicity of the environment and the unpredicted behaviors in the unbalanced relationship of my parents are the reasons I haven't had the conversation with my mother. I'd admit that my memories at the age of five years are still vivid and alive in some instances, though I buried them deep within my sub-conscious mind. On the other hand, at the height of my self-awareness in truth, I have come to know that unresolved issues are impediments from manifesting what the heart desires. Nevertheless, we were immersed in the stories about my first early days and it was time to wrap up the conversation so I could meditate before entering into the dream spaces and resting my avatar. Mom said, "Kiss the girls for me and I love y'all. Good night," and I responded with all my love and then our talk had ended.

There was much stillness and quietness in the air that I could have sworn that I had seen the essence of silence with a shadow. My body was frozen in place, but my thoughts kept moving around the fact that I was a happy and free going child, who always loved to run. So, I assumed that explains my active lifestyle today, the number of 5k and 10k runs I have participated in, and my athletic abilities, that I had greatly demonstrated in high school sports, mainly in basketball and in track. Moreover, another defining moment in self-discovery is that I was a curious child who wanted to learn everything, which I still can attest to that fact. So what could it be that is pinning me down or am I sabotaging myself? Am I not an unlimited being? Who imposed these limits on me? And with whom am I wrestling with or what am I allowing into my life that is delaying this unexplainable satisfaction and fulfillment that my heart and soul seek? I shall continue in this discovery mode until I can substantiate and make sense out of the path that I feel I have been stuck on. Apparently, there's a lesson I haven't yet grasped, although I have been adamant about ending that cycle. It's one thing to be a child and not have any control of the situations and circumstances and another damn thing to be of adult age and living as if I have no control over the matters, operating and responding in the same matter as I once did as a child. Nevertheless, what can you do when you have not been taught? So, I'd say that one must leave the familiar places and faces and adventure off to explore and seek to find a wise and harmonic way of living.

Chapter 2

BROKEN

Oh goodness, it's midnight and I have not gathered my meditation items and placed them in my sacred area to spend time with Higher Self. This will help clear my thoughts so I may have a well-rested night, the burning of sage to clear the space of any negative energies lurking around, the sounds of 432 Hertz frequency, and a glass of alkaline mineralized water in my reach, if needed. Within five minutes into the meditation, the voice within lets me know that I still had hidden fears and pains that needed to be uncovered and confronted with. In the meantime, I believed that my mind has a brain of its own because it totally ignored that thought and wandered off to another time and space that I once occupied when I traveled to Sao Paulo, Brazil, at that time I was enrolled in a graduate study abroad program in the summer of 2009. I assumed my body and mind were recreating the feelings that I experienced in those moments when I stepped foot on the grounds of Sao Paulo. It was that feeling that I had been there in past times, so much so that I recalled feeling as if the grounds had recognized my unique footprints. In fact, a jolt of energy moved from the soles of my feet directly to my heart and I brewed in such joy, warmth, and excitement. Nevertheless, our group sought out to visit a number of places like corporate businesses, financial stock markets, and government entities. However, my heart was exceedingly glad to have spent much time in the street markets where all the vendors made authentic crafts, arts, and cooked healthy meals. I remembered being so overwhelmed with what my eyes witnessed and not to mention, I was astonished at how well I blended in with the natives there. Indeed, it was a melting pot of beautiful beings of different shades and there seem to be no color filters on who partners with who, as supposed to the racism and discrimination stuff that heavily penetrates the media in the United States. However, I noticed the "haves and have nots" are another way that the country identifies its natives. Finally, I was touched by the harmony and unity within the families as they were combining their own individual uniqueness and offering their gifts to the world and creating wealth, living a balanced lifestyle aligned with the natural way as it should be. At least, that is the story I gathered from my brief visit to that foreign land.

Suddenly, it dawned on me that I'd rather not confront the truths of the matter in what I am struggling with internally, and clearly, I was not focused on mediating since I was invaded by those memories which I cherished. I could not sit in silence, so I started to journal. My spirit was having another delicate moment and I needed to listen to its voice and I wrote:

The truth of the matter is, you have been hurt by those who have been the closest to you. You are a gentle old soul, loyal and true, and unfortunately, many can see this light, but their intentions are not always innocent in most cases. You are the kind of being who will give your time and energy in every way to come to the aid of those in need and to those who you know little about their true intentions. Because of the trust you hold so dearly to them, you have been blindly succumbing to their aid, and as a result, you then suffered emotionally, mentally, and financially. So however the energy is being exchanged, whether, good or bad, balanced or unbalanced, the same energy flow continues and bleeds into your adult life, personal relationships, and even certain job situations. In other words, those repetitive behaviors and characteristics of those taking advantage of your light create the same patterns to the next lesson that you entered, which is the same lesson in disguise. The reason is, you have not passed its exams. For instance, the marriage and the divorce, and then the new-found love you had are all the same. Needless to say, those relationships reflect how you are internally in your relationship with thy self. Although, in your ignorance, you just were not aware that forming and nurturing a relationship with thy self should be your first priority in every way! Due to your upbringing and its inherited conditioning, the focal point was survival; the worries of not consistently having the basic essentials and genuine care, in addition to the lack of balance and harmony in the environments you dwelled. So, why would you think that your adult life would be any different than your early developmental years? If you don't know how to fix what is broken, then it would be left still broken. You may seek out ways on how to repair, but how do you know what to seek and what tools would actually be effective in repairing you? Otherwise, you will continue to attract other broken parts or pieces which come forward in the form of your personal relationships, jobs, and social circles! Why would a fixed person want anything or anyone that is broken? In order to attract a sense of wholeness into your life and personal relationships and so on, first, you must possess a sense of wholeness in the relationship with thy self. Howbeit, would you be able to recognize in someone or things that sense of wholeness? Notwithstanding the fact that the Universe puts back in front of you that which you need to fix, and in this case, it is you, my love! You gotta fix you!

In a nutshell, my spirit is crying out to gain from life that which has been freely given unto the unlimited being that I am. Yet, I struggle with grasping and retaining whatever I quench for. How can I be angry at the lessons that are coming my way? They are just doing what they came to do. Even in my retrospective analysis, I still do not know what lesson I'm in today! Only possessing knowledge is not sufficient to fulfill a dream into a living reality; therefore, one must combine actions along with the thoughts and desires at the same time to make those dreams a living reality. Moreover, these truths revealed warrant a quest to explore with the assumption that taking a spiritual transformation journey is a pre-requisite to manifest my heart's desires. I trust that there's an overflow of abundance designated for me, but it seems as though it requires me to heal and resurrect unto the limited-less being of that of my soul's origin. Somewhere above or below where I came from, this magical place gifted me with such intuitive thoughts. Thus, I have always felt an omnipresence surrounding me whenever I engaged with my thoughts on paper, expressing myself to the God and Goddess I suppose. Interestingly, they both simultaneously respond with these crafted words because I write these sayings so effortlessly. Evidently, the awareness that I have come forward into is that professional growth is not the same as spiritual and personal development growth. If the former is not balanced with the latter, then the personal life will suffer tremendously, and honestly, those unnecessary hardships really could have been avoided or lessened.

Chapter 3

THE INHERITED CONDITIONING

I am angry! My soul is not pleased, as it mourns over the I AM that it does not know. How can I come to know myself now that I am aware? Where do I begin? Who am I? I am not my mother's child. I am not my father's child. How can I be of someone or persons when they do not know the I AM within themselves? By and large, my "monkey mind" is definitely overactive and I am starting to feel exhausted from all of these questions that birthed more questions than I can quickly find answers to. By the same token, a profound thought I pondered on was whether or not that the I AM buried itself so that I could not find it. Hence, I come forward onto an inner journey to release the sufferings, pains, grief, and anger that once hindered the I AM from experiencing this gift of life as a free limited-less being.

I meditated for days on this new awareness I was becoming conscious of, and the next day, I decided to go for a ride. Not too long into the driving, I was met with the pouring rainfall. I kept driving anyway because I needed to leave those four walls and sit with Nature near the main artery that brings life into the city, the Mississippi River. It is one of the major conduits that lead to the center of Mother Earth's heartbeats. Meanwhile, the rain sounds grew harder and louder as I approached the Harbor Town River Walk Park, and I gave thanks for being safely nested and comforted in Mother's womb called Earth. Within a few minutes of observing the different patterns of the current flow in the river, I began to wail. I felt so lost again but above all, I needed to purge those toxic emotions, so the intensity of my cries were announced bluntly into the heavens, expressing themselves respectfully to a god who apparently has not been paying any attention to the circumstances I've encountered. Shortly, thereafter, I gained my composure. I assumed that I went through a cleansing process because I started to feel renewed. The rain still poured and it was best to stay parked until the heavily saturated clouds moved the precipitation farther west of the state. In the meantime, I pulled out my cellular device to browse the Internet and found a YouTube video with two wise gentlemen speaking on the topic "The Spiritual Meaning of Relationships." The guest on the show is a Metaphysician and the host is a Relationship Coach and TV/Radio Personality. Their conversations flowed and the interview questions were all intriguing, so I was locked into listening to the two hour recording. Then half way into the video, there it was. **The BIG QUESTION! "IS THE CONDITIONING DOING THE CHOOSING?"** And, I thought; that's a loaded gun for sure. So then, I took notes and meditated on that conversation for days.

Needless to say, I began to distill the knowledge that I was coming into, so I took my journal and wrote:

The life you were born into applied a form of conditioning. Your conditioning is the family traditions, inherited beliefs, philosophies, and values; environments you have been exposed to and dwelled in; the systems – government, school, religion, media, and history – all designed to condition you against your divine nature. So the question here is, then who am I really? Everything is up for questioning! Who is the oppressor thinks that it is by imposing its conditions on me? Coming forward, stripping away all the layers of conditioning brings me back around to my divine spirit, and in silence, I meditate on the voice inside, where the Goddess and the God of Divine speak. The very things that I questioned surely are the same things some of our ancestors struggled with; though in their times they just accepted the way the conditioning was delivered and handed down. This is the reason you have questioned things because you have inherited your ancestors' desires to find these things to free not only your mind, but the minds of the ancestors who were once held captive or are still held in captivity.

I was awakened by the sunshine smiling upon me as if it was proud of me rising to the calling to seek out those missing pieces of the puzzle that would bring me to a sense of wholeness. I noticed that the pen was still in my hand, realizing that I dozed off while writing some profound thoughts that came out of the four corners of a barren living room that could truly use some exciting decorations and inviting colors. Nevertheless, I had the idea to go on a road trip despite the travel restrictions imposed on the populations to lessen their physical contact and social connections due to this contagious disease that is causing sickness to the people. Not that I am nonchalant, but I have my own problems to solve. If I were to focus my energy on bringing about a resolution for myself, surely I will be positioned to assist others. So off to the beach I go. I'm heading east. Acting with spontaneity is the attitude I now have adopted.

Riding into the sunrise on interstate 40 at 7:33 a.m., listening to the singer *Sheryl Crow, Soak Up The Sun* with the sunroof back and my natural tresses blowing freely raises my spirit to the highest. It makes me feel so alive, carefree, and happy. Unfortunately, I had not been aware that this is the feeling I needed to give to myself, when unconsciously in past relationships, I sought out those grandiose feelings in my partner, which resulted in being disappointed every time. I now come into the knowing that it is up to me to fortify the love relationship with thy self and stand on that firm foundation before I open myself up to receive another champion's love and energy. I concluded that our combined love energies will only stand as strong as the love that is within me and that strength will determine our fate. Nevertheless, it is still early daylight hours while driving along greenery scenic views, and it is likened to engaging in meditation sitting still, but with movement and alertness. I extended the sun-visor to enhance my visuals of the road and the traffic, but it was not enough. The sun rays were beaming sharply through the windshield to ensure that I absorb the upload of its information, further delighting my impromptu journey. As if I was receiving a message from my spirit guide about the location of the I AM that I am seeking, moreover, a feeling of relief overwhelmed me, leaving behind the environment and work, and the mundane routines on repeat as exhausting as they can be. On the other hand, the thought of driving for twelve hours should be discouraging, but I was more than ever energized to explore and shake up the routine.

Over four hundred miles of traveling from the corner of West Tennessee towards eastern Tennessee, where it borders North Carolina is the first adventurous road trip I have taken alone, even though it was not my first time driving from corner to corner in Tennessee. Fast approaching was the state line of North Carolina, to the city of Asheville, the highway signs warned me, and I noticed the traffic flow was heavy and sailing at a reasonable pace as if the travelers were actually obeying the speed limits. The eighteen-wheeler trucks were in a single filed line coasting steadily as the grades of the elevations grew steeper I observed. Having a CB radio to listen in on what the truckers are saying and the information they are sharing from base would have been a great asset to assist me in navigating the unfamiliar roadways, but I had to take heed to their flow and follow suit. In a distance, there were speechless views of mountain ranges extending their reach where the clouds scrolled, crossing over the territory, and the endless acres of land and a few homes built at higher elevations on the mountains I surveyed. Suddenly, the smell of rubber tires invaded my air space and the sounds of screeching tires ahead immediately warned me to signal and move over to the farthest lane away from the scene. As I was passing by, I quickly noticed the truck driver had skillfully handled the descent of the grade. It finally dawned on me that I had entered the Appalachian Mountain ranges and the depths and valleys are likened to meeting the Supreme Being. Nevertheless, I felt a higher presence, and I then became a deaf person and there are no words in the English language to properly describe these feelings of the omnipresence. This wondrous road trip is one to tackle during the high peak hours of the sunlight. I definitely would not attempt to travel in the late-night hours during a new moon, yet I can imagine settling into and staying in a cabin overnight nested within the mountain range under a full moon, and how amazing that would be. Surely, that is the honeymoon of a lifetime to have with thy self and the Creator and that is definitely an idea worth pursuing!

I passed the central part of North Carolina, and I must admit that driving for twelve hours with only two restroom stops is overly ambitious. I laughed, thinking that perhaps it was my ego driving as well. On a few past adventures with family, I have been ridiculed for creating an itinerary for vacationing; and going on a whim, well, I could really use some directions, so I continued traveling east on the interstate until I spotted a traveler's rest stop to gather maps and coupons for food and hotels. Browsing through the pamphlets and maps, I was not pleased with the food or hotel options. I then had the thoughts of camping on the beach and finding a local natural grocery store to grab some life-force energy foods that would serve me. I quickly shopped for the foods and supplies I needed to camp under the stars and the sounds of the ocean waves because the night was swiftly fading the daylight away. According to the State of North Carolina's roadmap, there are a number of beaches to choose from; Emerald Isle, Wrightsville Beach, and Sunset Beach just to name a few. I intended to camp out at the closest beach, but at that point, I was very exhausted and hungry, so I stayed out overnight in my van at a gas station and servicing truck center to rest. I have ample spacing in the van to spread out when the seats are folded down, allowing me to prepare a lite sandwich of spouted wheat berry bread with almond butter and sliced bananas on top and mango slices as a side dish. It was very satisfying. I then watched the traffic volume flowing through the servicing station until my eyes could not keep watching.

The next day, the shape of the sun at 5:55 a.m appeared so massive in the sky, emitting the energy colors of orange and red so violently, and peaceful at the same time. I marveled at the sun's grand entrance into the day, realizing that the Earth's rotation process in its relation to the Equator is the reason for the sun's enormous shape when it's on the horizon - I don't know, it's my speculation! It was another three hours to Sunset Beach in North Carolina with no plans to a retail shop, whereas I would have shopped at all the outlets and found the best local eateries. Believe it or not, I had no interest in any of these things for the external pleasures no longer were appealing while I journey forward to a sense of wholeness and balance. I finally arrived at Sunset Beach; its tinted light brownish and whitish sands and its endless shoreline view of the Atlantic Ocean was welcoming. I spent my entire day receiving an upload of food directly from The Source of Light, but also I was careful not to get sunburned. As the night drew nigh, I gathered my tent and food supplies from the van and located nearby a camping spot adjacent to the bridge walk that seem to be held by hundreds of utility street poles slightly over a quarter-mile long. Nevertheless, the sky gracefully illumined with stars, planets, satellites, and other airspace entities that I am not familiar with. And of course, the season brings the Gemini constellation in full force which is outlined and configured strongly in the night on a full moon. Such beauty and magnificent power surrounded me. Surely, the very thing we search for is not hidden because God is ubiquitous. And if we say that is true, then we can also say that God is within us. However, in my opinion, I think many search externally for a God that is hidden within one's self. Since I have removed myself from familiar places and faces, away from the distractions, I can now hear so much that makes common sense and truth to me. Nevertheless, the Atlantic Ocean waves grow twice their size at night than during the day, and the tides reaches farther north onto the land at night. Also, the sea creatures were starting to invade my tent and I initially thought it would be a great idea to commune with the elements until I realized that I had not blinked my eyes nor yearned, and I started to feel hesitation within my body telling me that we're not so ready yet. I then noticed the time at 11:11 p.m and took that as my sign to pack up my belongings and continue with camping the nights out in my hotel on wheels.

Another day had come and gone and driving along the Southeastern Atlantic coastal lines to different beaches in North Carolina and nearby bordering South Carolina, it was time to contact my brother and his family in Fayetteville, NC, because I needed a warm bath and a home-cooked meal. They were elated to welcome me over to join in on the family night of camping in their backyard, roasting s'mores, and dancing to salsa and samba. Even though I had my share of outdoor and salt life, it is more in-joyable exploring with loved ones; however, at times, it is required that one ventures off and come to terms with thy self and circumstances.

I must be off to my next destination heading west to the northern part of Whidbey Island, Washington, where the Whidbey Island Naval Air Station is located. The airline tickets were offered as low as $150.00 round trip due to the global pandemic.

Certainly, I would continue to take the necessary precautions, but how is one to live freely if at every moment you are listening to the news and other media outlets that consistently creates fear; thus, having many feeling lost and confused. By minding my own business and focusing on my well-being, I would be able to take advantage of the opportunities in the present moment. Anyway, I truly enjoyed nesting in a comfortable bed and creating quality memories with family, but I must continue in my ebb and flow and they agreed that I may leave my van parked at their home until I returned. I arrived at the Raleigh airport like a breeze. The traffic was light and definitely, this thing has changed things; the airport was not overcrowded and the lines were fairly doable to stand in. I was off onto another part of my Lewis and Clarke adventure I thought, flying over a plethora of mountains that I learned about in geography classes, but I cannot recall their names at this moment. I tried contacting my aunt and uncle to inform them that I will be arriving by flight into the State of Washington to visit Whidbey Island, but I got distracted by the coverings of snow resting on the summit of the mountains, which seems like the snow tops were disappearing, and they were starting to look like an endless bowl of Oreo cookies from 35,000 feet in altitude. I then felt the tightening in my stomach and realized that I needed to close the window shades, and how funny is it, that almost everybody wants the view at the top, but is one able to handle the changes in the air pressure? Darn, I cannot make a phone call, but I can send air messages for an additional fee, of course. I then texted my aunt to inform her of my adventures and needless to say, she responded in bewilderment that I was traveling during these times, yet, she still welcomed to accommodate my arrival. Shortly thereafter, I landed in Tacoma, WA, after six and a half hours of surveying the foundation of the heavens. I was so happy to finally be on the grounds! The conversations with The Creator will have to continue another time. I was very satisfied with the arrangements of the Delta's aircraft, as the seats in the middle of all the rows were not occupied, which gave me ample spacing to relax in comfort. Then the flight attendants announced that the aircraft updated its air filters for better air quality and flow along with a sanitized aircraft. Without a doubt, I picked a great time to take flight!

I took heed to the instructions that my aunt sent to me and I needed to take a bus north towards Mukilteo, which is nearby the Lighthouse Park where I'll board the Mukilteo Ferry. I was expected to cross the Puget Sound body of waters, while they await my arrival there to pick me up. Sitting near the front entrance of the bus while the driver heads north on interstate 5, these indescribable scenery views are just as indescribable as the scenery views above in 37,000 feet of altitude. Such beauty of Mother Earth surrounds me and the Universe commends me for my bravery and courage, so it continued to reveal so much life to me; and I then felt the fire energy within my body propelling me to move forward onto claiming my birthright as a limited-less and free being no matter what's going on around me. After an hour drive to the ferry and boarding the dock, I sailed onto Whidbey Island and joined with my relatives, spending some quality time, listening to "down home blues" oldie music, and laughing so much so that we were overwhelmed with joy in every way!

Furthermore, there were days that I explored the outdoors alone; a nearby community in which I surveyed was like a replica of the small town Humboldt, Tennessee, as I was becoming familiar with its territory. Hiking towards the Puget Sounds, I was engrossed by the ocean and lakes flowing between the Cascade Mountains and the Olympia Mountains. These wonders are magnificent! It is also amazing that even the smallest life in the deep waters are taken care of, and the groups of seagulls fly onto the sandy shores to rest their pretty ivory wings and to hold space as if they were meditating on their next landing spot or meal. The ocean blue-greenish waters are ever clear that I had the visibility to witness the sea life and how they were winking back at me. I became overwhelmed with joy in discovering the pink, brown, and yellow starfish. I felt like a child again! I was playful with neither worries nor thoughts of those troubling situations back at home, and suddenly, the ocean waves pounded upon the rock cliffs in juxtaposition to the bridge walk, so I assumed they heard me. I stood frozen in those moments, realizing the luxury that comes packaged with being a resident on this island and the beauty of the tides washing onto shore the tree logs, scattering them up to lay as dining tables to hold the wine glasses for couples' romance at the seashore. I then felt speechless and my body was so loose that it became fragile, smiling more than usual as I stood balanced in the palm of Mother Earth's hands. The mountains I was sandwiched between on the east and west emitted this essence of protection. The day started to cease, so I decided that I should head back in time for dinner. As I continued, I saw a billboard about visiting the mountain at Mount Shasta, California, also known as a sacred spot for seekers on a spiritual journey, allowing them to connect directly with the root chakra of Mother Earth and fortifying the relationship with their higher selves. At this point on my quest, I eliminated the word coincidence and I began trusting the process. So, I booked a flight to Mt. Shasta and informed my relatives that I must be on my way the next early dawn and their hospitality was heartfelt. I expressed my gratitude as they helped me to create such cherishing memories.

Chapter 4

RECOVERED

So my tales of adventure continued with an exploration to the city of Mount Shasta, California! My airline ticket was only $72.00 for a one-way trip. I arrived at the airport in Redding, CA, then I traveled by bus into the city. I had no plans and guidance as to how I would reach the wondrous spiritual grounds at the base of the mountain, so I searched online for tourist information. But due to the global health confusion, not many businesses were conducting tours, or at least some of them didn't even update their availability online. When I arrived into the city, I felt a sense of wholeness and

I noticed some of its residents were all delighted and freely moving on with life as supposed to some people I witnessed in bigger cities that I had traveled to. On the other hand, the people dwelling in Mt. Shasta seem balanced, perhaps, being adjacent to Weed City might have something to do with it — then laughter consumed me as I was reflecting on a past memory that my dad would jokingly say *you can believe what you want to believe, that is on you!* So, it is unfortunate that these fearful tactics were exploding all around the world using different media outlets, and many of the people had begun falling prey to them. Nonetheless, I was elated to witness the residents of this city moving right along still enjoying life. Instantly, I was distracted by the conversation of a tour guide who was speaking to a crowd of 19 people and they were strapped with gear ready to hike the mountains and needed to be on their way to reach its base and also view the summit of the mountain by 11:44 a.m. The clouds would then heavily saturate and cover the air spaces hiding the views, so they also needed to make haste to their camping spot onto the mountain by 2:22 p.m. The tour guide started on his way in leading the group and then he faced them quickly to inform them that there were zero cases of this thing in the city of Mount Shasta. Of course, I was eavesdropping into their conversations, trying to disguise myself as a local, but surely having a carry-on bag with wheels labeled me as a tourist. Right there, I concluded that I'll have to circle back to Mt. Shasta another time to explore the mountain since I was not prepared as the hikers were well equipped to endure the rugged terrain and the unpredictable changes in the weather that the tour guide spoke of.

Next, I began to locate the farmers' markets and CBD dispensaries, but I was quickly distracted by a Shaman and the rhythm beats in the 432 Hertz frequency emitting these energies from his drums, hypnotizing me and directing the soles of my shoes in his path. When I reached within 6 feet of space between us, he then immediately stopped the sounds and welcomed me. Then, he introduced himself and spoke on many great things about living in the city, and he also shared how he hiked Mount Shasta during his awakening and that his spiritual journey strongly continues over 40 years. Without a doubt, I felt a sense of safety being entertained in his space and I preceded to also share a few of my life experiences. But he then inquired of my birth date and described the astrological aspects of the planets' positioning in the Universe on that date I was birthed. He explained how the ancestors from thousands of years ago had the chance to study the constellation and use the stars as a map to foretell the changes in the season and for agricultural purposes, in addition to, studying the patterns of the personalities and characteristics traits of the new beings birthed on different dates and times. Nonetheless, all things happened in perfect alignment. I trust that the Universe revealed these things because I set out to follow my heart. So in other words, I was open-minded to receive the message from the wise elder. He noticed the countenance on my face was exceedingly glad for the knowledge, so the Shaman continued and stated, "There's a bit of world based heaviness that will be released by your pursuit of ideas and things that will uplift your spirit. There seems to be something within you that is screaming to come out or in fact burst out. Whatever this truly is, it is what will allow you to achieve levels of self-satisfaction and internal happiness that has not been seen previously, and if it has been seen in the past, it was only a small glimpse into what is truly possible." I respectfully inquired to the Shaman how he was able to gather those insights and he replied that my aura energy field which surrounds the body emits this frequency and he knew I would also be delighted to receive this knowledge.

Truly, we were lost in time and conversation, and suddenly, the positioning of the sun's rays reflecting on my face signaled me to be on my way to find overnight sleeping accommodation. I then expressed my gratefulness and ended our talk. I walked over to a nearby gas servicing station to purchase a few snacks and souvenirs, and to grab a free map of the city and tourist guides containing information on places to dine and stay. I then surveyed the area for other modes of transportation rather than walking. I noticed a bus stop across the way with a signpost on the utility pole detailed the days and times of the bus arrival, so I made it in time to catch the last run of the day. In the meantime, I tried to keep myself busy by eating a small bag of dark chocolates with almonds and listening to a chill music mix on YouTube. However, my thoughts had the conversation with the Shaman on replay the entire time while waiting on the bus to arrive. The scenic views of the mountains were very enticing to the point of contemplating the relocation of my family near a mountain range. I truly felt at ease and light on my feet and these fuzzy feelings of happiness and excitement brewed profusely. Indeed, I've grasped the meaning of having 2020 vision in the year 2020. And why this was the perfect time to go in, the year awakens one to gain insights about one's self to raise self-awareness and to create and form a vision for their future which would then inspire one into action. Consequently, I even might testify to these truths to encourage others to go within. Peeling the layers off from the emotional baggage and coming into a brand new me, I likened it to that of the Earth evolving into a new age, as it might seem to others on that early spring day when the Earth stood still and held its breath. Finally, the bus arrived, I took my seat near the front entrance as I normally would do and I was off to stay overnight at a reasonable priced hotel, considering the fact that I had spent much of my savings on this journey. Nevertheless, this journey is priceless, and as a matter of fact, I now know that there are no endings, only that we come to a crossroads in life. Also, when faced with certain circumstances, major decisions have to be made, after all, it's insanity to continue the same. **For that reason, when one seeks out to expand and evolve, then the growth has to lead to more new beginnings, in which it takes wisdom to identify the demarcation between an ending being disguised as a new beginning and this cycle continues infinitely.**

A brand new day has arrived and the Delta airlines texted stating that my flight was on schedule. So, I wrapped up things at the hotel and caught the bus back to Redding, CA timely to get through security checkpoints and locate the terminal for boarding. It's funny how times are changing. I listened to the Delta representative called on the passengers who have seats in the rear of the aircraft to load onto the plane first, which reminded me of the biblical text about the "last shall be first." Again, I'd say what a great time to take flight! The plane was loaded to capacity at 60%, which was the new rule for limiting physical and social contact among the populations to minimize any risk of becoming ill associated with this global health crisis. The captain then came onto the speakers and announced that they were preparing for take-off and instructed the flight attendants to buckle into their assigned area seating. The engine sounds were growing louder and I closed my eyes as the plane gained such high speeds on the lift-off, and in my darkness were the colors red, yellow, orange, and green spinning as orbs. Needless to say, I smiled. I had thoughts that the energy from my chakras had started to re-opened and I embraced the moment. In the air communing with the clouds at 36,000 feet in altitude tell the story beneath on ground zero. The formation of the clouds truly tells the story of the Earth's grounds. Some cloud formations are like waterfalls, glaciers, mountains, and traffic patterns, and so on. I then noticed that the clouds had a number of groups that traveled together in different patterns of the current in the sky. Just as the rivers flow, the clouds too mimic their patterns of flow. Nevertheless, in my observations at altitude temperatures of -64, I then realized how I have always been connected with Source, The Creator. Exhaustion settled in and my body screamed for more rest. So, over the next five hours, I did just that until the scheduled connecting flight. My time spent in the sky was about the same amount of time spent on the road traveling, and after seven hours in the air, I plan to rest for a day at my brother's home before attempting to drive twelve hours back to West Tennessee.

Undoubtedly, I'll be returning home with a transformed mindset and renewed mental attitude, so I was more than ready for the road trip. Besides, the driving time goes by quickly once the unfamiliar territory has been explored. One of the many things to consider about traveling along a mountainous terrain is that the weather precipitation varies a lot and I can detect that by observing certain clouds patterns and the tinted greyish colored sky, warning me of the rainfall approaching in Asheville, NC. Then, I spotted a rainbow. As the rainbow was appearing closer, I tried to determine where the rainbow ended, and behold, the 7 colors arched over onto the interstate and I was exceedingly glad that I passed at the end of the rainbow for the first time ever! The realization that there's no end to a rainbow! I noticed how it penetrated the Earth's grounds bringing forth its light to shine in the underworld. So, even in darkness, the light will find its way to illuminate what is hidden. I then received a phone call that I was not going to answer while driving through this terrain, and it was a call that I have been ignoring for days from the love in my life. I assumed we are twin flames or have met in past lifetimes, and I have determined that we're on different paths in this lifetime. However, it would serve me to let go of any judgements about us because the efforts I put forth into becoming the greatest version of myself, what if, he is doing the same? Lastly, I must be focused on doing the work on myself because reality is like a movie projector, projecting everything that is happening internally with thy self, so I trust that the divine partnership that I desire that the Universe will bring forward in time.

Most importantly, composing my experiences of my inner journey to self-recovery would be a great publication and also sharing how I resurrected my true being to life. I then vividly recalled this billboard sign from some time ago and the message printed boldly for the public to read, "If your presence does not make an impact, then your absence won't make a difference." The Universe has spoken again unto me and it provided guidance on what I should be doing next. So, I guess it is time to retire temporarily from the workforce and engage in some creative writings. I finally arrived at my children god-parents' home and my girls ran and smothered me with hugs and smiles galore, and everyone was delighted I returned safely. We talked over an hour until my oldest child tugged on my shirt and said she was ready to go home. As we arrived into our residential housing complex and found parking, I noticed a familiar vehicle pulling alongside of me and surprisingly, I saw my love accompanied with countless balloons and a variety of flowers and roses, and we both were elated, so too, the children's faces were ever brighter in his presence. Yet, I never sent him any information on my whereabouts and I intentionally allowed his text messages and phone calls to go unanswered, because I just needed the space and time to journey within **to figure me out** before I could continue entertaining this love. I have made no commitment, in fact, I have reinstated my terms regarding the relationship in a humble matter, of course, and we both felt the feelings were mutual. Perhaps, I can say that I came forward from the journey fully recovered! Soon thereafter, being in the company of my girls and love, I then sensed the feelings of togetherness as we started anew in creating in-joyable moments. Thus, the next chapter begins **at a time to go in** with the visions to come forward in building a renewed legacy with a transformed mindset.

Epilogue

Elated about this new of way of living on the countryside with my love and children, we have several acres of land to grow gardens, raise livestock, and build additional footage onto the home for an office space. Rising with the sun and reflecting on these thoughts while my family continued resting, I freshen up for the day before heading outdoors to sit at the roots of the wisdom in the trees living in the backyard. I stared at them intently, examining their roots, branches, and leaves, wondering what were their worries? As tall as these trees stood, I wondered how long does a baby tree lives into its developing years before reaching adulthood, and how can it be determined when it has transitioned to an adult tree; and when it has become an elder?

Nevertheless, these trees have the advantage; they will always be connected to the wisdom of the elders as long as the elders are not uprooted from the earth.

As I continued in meditation, I then heard the spirit of the trees speaking, *"many of the children are not connected and they are not growing in the wisdom of the elders as these trees are. The year 2020 is the time to go in, and it gives back some time to the populace to mend, create and connect, deepening the family roots likening to that of these trees being grounded in the wisdom of its elders and Mother Earth."* I was overwhelmed with these truths revealed unto me, and they were facts about the current conditions of most children's spiritual development in today's society. I then felt a breeze across my shoulders and upper back as if the trees bended over to embrace me with a hug. Briefly, I sat in stillness and silence before ending my mediation.

I then took my shoes off and walked barefoot in order to connect deeply into the energy of Mother Earth while I explored the parameter of our home. I felt the sun's energy intensified and I began to feel much happier and loved! Then I heard my love called out to me and announced that breakfast was ready. He saw how my face was enlightened, and his curiosity lead him out to greet me, and my smile grew even wider and brighter. My jaw bone could not handle the pressure of such outer expressions of inner bliss! Furthermore, my love and I had no words to exchange. He had already read my mind and felt the essence of the love in our hearts. A certain indescribable feeling consumed me as if time had instantly paused in that moment of genuine love and admiration. His smile became brighter than mine, and we then embraced one another with a smothering hug, feeling the oneness of our spirits. We then heard in a near distance the laughter and giggle of our children, and as we were approaching the little voices, they ran to meet us and the baby girl said, "family hugs," and the oldest girl shouted, "squeeze me tighter!"

Living in these moments of being free is the paradise most of us have been waiting for. We think that it's the gaudy and fancy material possessions, but, in fact, it is as simply as rising with the sun and deciding to be content with a way of living that does not compromise a person's idea of what a balance and whole life looks and feels like to oneself. But, how can one come into this awareness? In my opinion, having a time out from an overstimulated routine, coupled with spending time with Mother Nature and expanding in self-love and self-knowledge aided me into some profound thoughts about the life I had been living and striving after. I then concluded that changing my focus from the external things and directing the energy towards finding a sense of wholeness and inner truth that I unknowingly planted seeds, resulting in attracting all that my heart and soul desire which they now spring forth effortlessly. In hindsight, it's most definitely not the external attainments, but it was that inner climb that I needed to hike, however, I was not familiar with the rugged terrain of my inner conditions. Indeed, it was a rough undertaking!

Unbeknownst to me, I was the treasure that I had been seeking and many of life challenges could have been avoided or lessen. But, where would I have acquired this knowledge and wisdom that I possess today? Consequently, I have changed my perspective about the type of life to live now that my sight has been renewed. Henceforth, would I be singing with the birds and feeling a sense of wholeness, gratitude and contentment when I rise each day forward. Without a doubt, hiking the mountain of self-discovery revealed many aspects about the life I was living which I needed to question, such as how I was raised to **be** and **live**. Basically, how I was raised to **believe**.

In conclusion, I have found that transforming your life requires a great deal of investment in self. The truth of the matter is that those life changes can lead one onto a journey of enlightenment and spiritual transformation. Unfortunately, I had discovered that I was living out of harmony with my highest self and had failed to listen to my inner voice callings to align my way of thinking and living accordingly. I had been operating under a projected image not that of my true self in which the false self was created and shaped by the environment, traditions, philosophies, and beliefs that I was born into. Coupling all those experiences lead me to take the journey granted by **the gift of time** which allowed me to seek out a balanced way of living. Having that **time to go in,** and expand on self-love and self-knowledge resulted in experiencing a mental breakthrough. It was like scales falling from my eyes! The internal pains that I meekly once endured mentally, emotionally and physically, I no longer felt heavy nor burdened. What an amazing inner journey to undertake with this gift of time at *A Time To Go In*!

www.ingramcontent.com/pod-product-compliance
Lightning Source LLC
Chambersburg PA
CBHW052034260626
47163CB00006B/300